COOL CARS

FERRARI 812 SUPERFAST

BY NATHAN SOMMER

EPIC

BELLWETHER MEDIA ››› MINNEAPOLIS, MN

EPIC BOOKS are no ordinary books. They burst with intense action, high-speed heroics, and shadows of the unknown. Are you ready for an Epic adventure?

This edition first published in 2023 by Bellwether Media, Inc.

No part of this publication may be reproduced in whole or in part without written permission of the publisher. For information regarding permission, write to Bellwether Media, Inc. Attention: Permissions Department, 6012 Blue Circle Drive, Minnetonka, MN 55343.

Library of Congress Cataloging-in-Publication Data

LC record for Ferrari 812 Superfast available at: https://lccn.loc.gov/2022020236

Text copyright © 2023 by Bellwether Media, Inc. EPIC and associated logos are trademarks and/or registered trademarks of Bellwether Media, Inc.

Editor: Kieran Downs   Designer: Jeffrey Kollock

Printed in the United States of America, North Mankato, MN

TABLE OF CONTENTS

TRACK MEETS ROAD	**4**
ALL ABOUT THE 812 SUPERFAST	**6**
PARTS OF THE 812 SUPERFAST	**12**
THE 812 SUPERFAST'S FUTURE	**20**
GLOSSARY	**22**
TO LEARN MORE	**23**
INDEX	**24**

TRACK MEETS ROAD »

A driver starts her Ferrari 812 Superfast. The engine roars as it turns on. She steers it onto the street.

The car rounds a curve. The driver feels a rush. The 812 Superfast makes everyday driving feel like the track!

ALL ABOUT THE 812 SUPERFAST

ENZO FERRARI

FERRARI SF1000 FORMULA 1 CAR

> Ferrari was founded by driver Enzo Ferrari. Its first car came out in 1947. Ferrari has won the most **Formula 1** races of any company.

Ferraris are known for their **luxury**. Famous **models** include the F40, 250 GTO, and 365 GTB/4.

A HISTORY-MAKING SALE

A Ferrari 250 GTO sold for around $70 million in 2018. This was the most expensive car sale ever!

250 GTO

The 812 Superfast first came out in 2017. It replaced the F12 model.

The 812 Superfast has Ferrari's strongest engine. It can reach 60 miles (97 kilometers) per hour in 2.8 seconds!

2017 812 SUPERFAST

812 SUPERFAST BASICS

YEAR FIRST MADE — 2017

COST — starts at $335,000

HOW MANY MADE — more than 5,000

FEATURES

V12 engine

rear diffuser

electric power steering

The 812 Superfast is one of Ferrari's fastest road cars ever. It speeds up to 211 miles (340 kilometers) per hour!

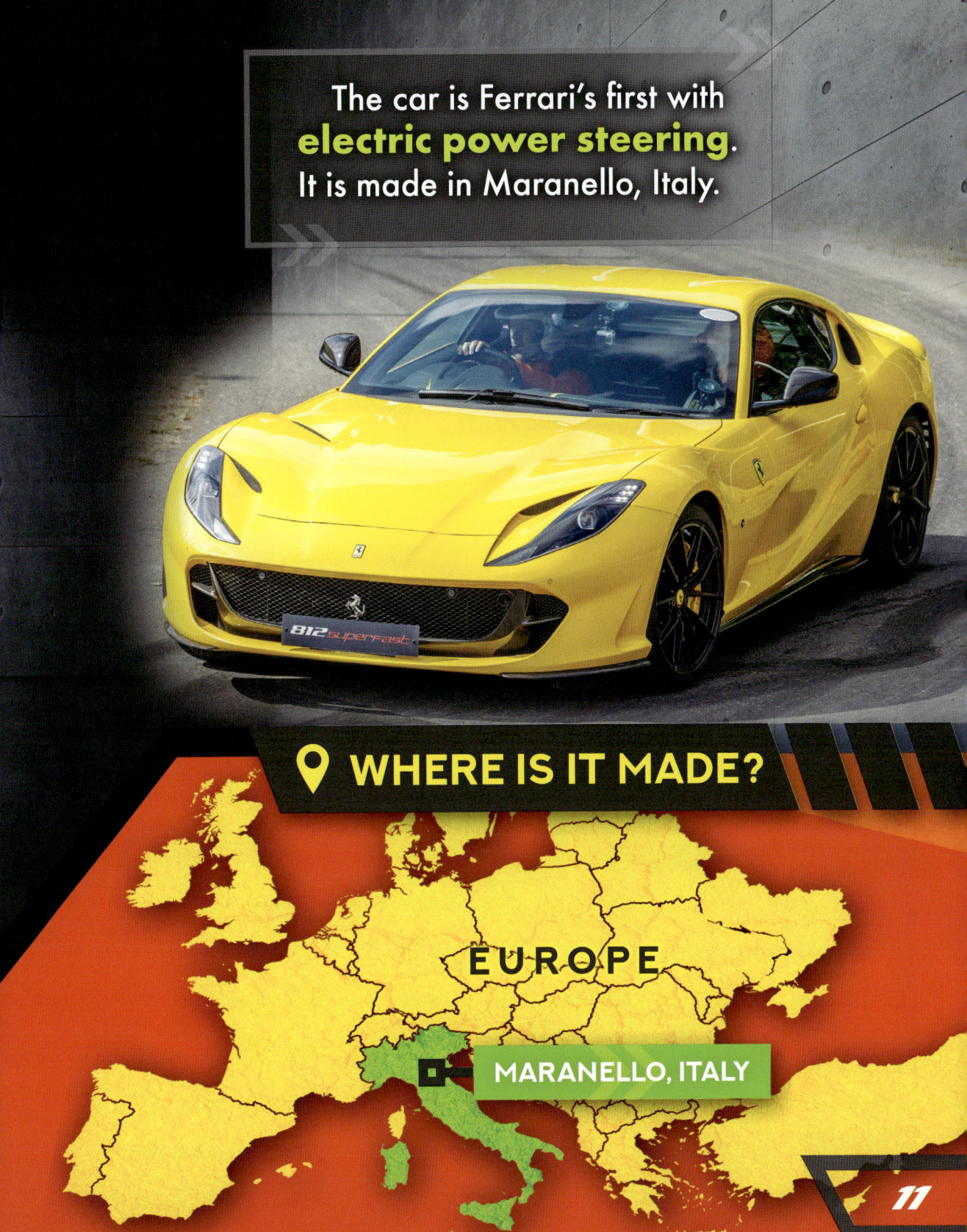

The car is Ferrari's first with **electric power steering**. It is made in Maranello, Italy.

WHERE IS IT MADE?

EUROPE

MARANELLO, ITALY

PARTS OF THE 812 SUPERFAST »

The 812 Superfast has a powerful **V12 engine**. It sits under the car's long hood.
The car has a **dual-clutch transmission**. This helps the engine change gears.

🛠 ENGINE SPECS

6.5-LITER V12

TOP SPEED	211 miles (340 kilometers) per hour
0-60 TIME	2.8 seconds
HORSEPOWER	789 hp

The 812 Superfast has vents. They make the car **aerodynamic**. In front are **LED** headlights. **Air intakes** cool the engine.

AIR INTAKE

LED HEADLIGHT

 SIZE CHART

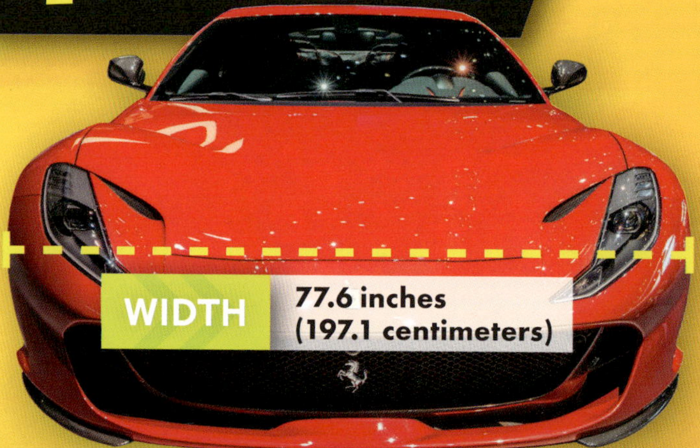

WIDTH 77.6 inches (197.1 centimeters)

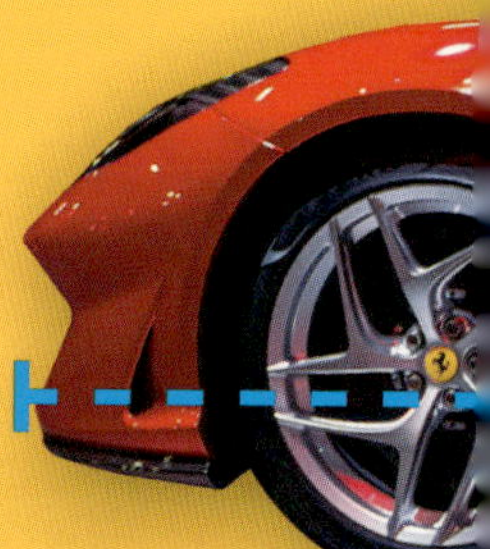

The back has four **tailpipes**. It also has a **rear diffuser**. This opens at high speeds.

REAR DIFFUSER

TAILPIPES

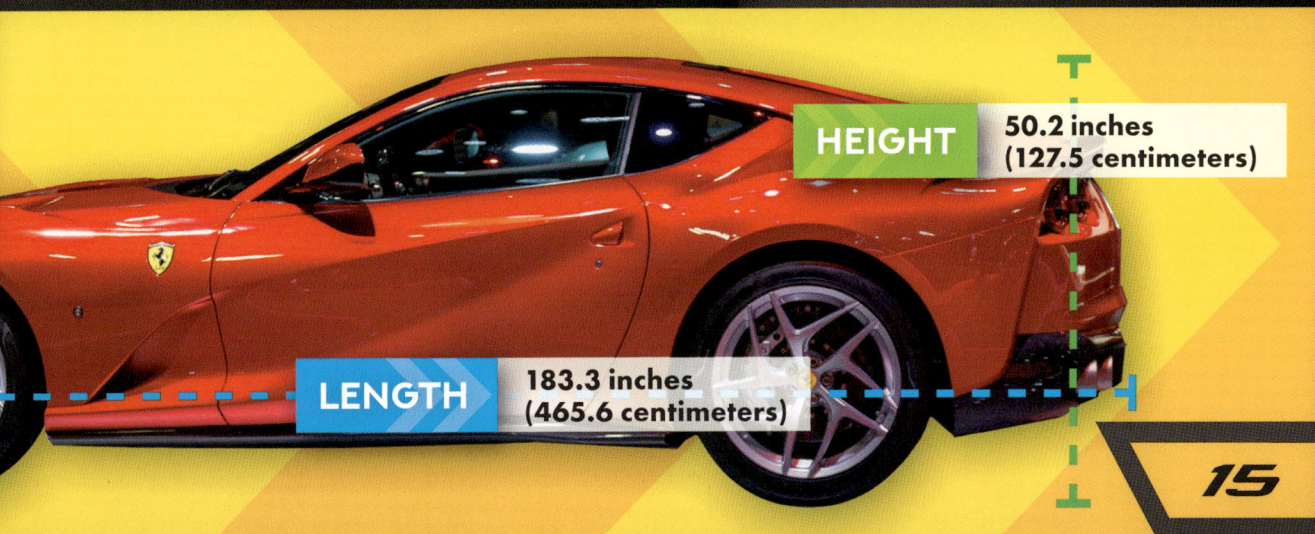

HEIGHT 50.2 inches (127.5 centimeters)

LENGTH 183.3 inches (465.6 centimeters)

15

The 812 Superfast seats two people.
It has more space than most sports cars.

Drivers choose the color and pattern of the seats. They can connect their iPhones to the car for maps and music.

SPECIAL STEERING WHEEL

The 812 Superfast has buttons on its steering wheel. These include controls for the windshield wipers and turn signals.

There are different models of the 812 Superfast. The 812 Competizione is a **coupe** model. It has an even stronger engine!

ONE POPULAR CAR

Ferrari only built 1,598 Competizione models. The car sold out very quickly.

812 COMPETIZIONE

812 GTS

The 812 GTS model is a **convertible**. Its roof can fold back.

THE 812 SUPERFAST'S FUTURE »

Ferrari stopped taking orders for the 812 Superfast in 2022. But the company will make more cars with V12 engines. The Ferrari 812 Superfast is a special sports car. It lives up to its Superfast name!

GLOSSARY

aerodynamic—able to move through air easily

air intakes—openings on a car that allow air to reach its engine

convertible—a car with a folding or soft roof

coupe—related to a type of car with a hard roof and two doors

dual-clutch transmission—a car part that has two clutches and changes gears automatically; a clutch is the part of a car that moves power from the engine to the wheels.

electric power steering—a system that uses an electric motor to control the steering wheel

Formula 1—an international car racing series

LED—related to lights that save energy and take a very long time to burn out

luxury—great pleasure or comfort

models—specific kinds of cars

rear diffuser—a part on the back underside of a car that directs air and makes the car more aerodynamic

tailpipes—pipes used to direct gases from a car's engine out of the engine and away from the car

V12 engine—an engine with 12 cylinders arranged in the shape of a "V"

TO LEARN MORE

AT THE LIBRARY

Albino, Dustin. *Superfast Formula 1 Racing*. Minneapolis, Minn.: Lerner Publications, 2020.

Smith, Ryan. *Ferrari*. New York, N.Y.: AV2, 2021.

Sommer, Nathan. *Ferrari F8 Tributo*. Minneapolis, Minn.: Bellwether Media, 2023.

ON THE WEB

FACTSURFER

Factsurfer.com gives you a safe, fun way to find more information.

1. Go to www.factsurfer.com.

2. Enter "Ferrari 812 Superfast" into the search box and click 🔍.

3. Select your book cover to see a list of related content.

INDEX

250 GTO, 7
812 Competizione, 18
812 GTS, 19
air intakes, 14
basics, 9
company, 6, 8, 10, 11, 18, 20
convertible, 19
coupes, 18
dual-clutch transmission, 12
electric power steering, 11
engine, 4, 8, 12, 14, 18, 20
engine specs, 12
Ferrari, Enzo, 6
Formula 1, 6
headlights, 14
history, 6, 7, 8, 20
iPhones, 17
Maranello, Italy, 11
models, 7, 8, 18, 19

rear diffuser, 15
roof, 19
seats, 16, 17
size, 14–15
speed, 8, 10, 15
steering wheel, 17
tailpipes, 15
vents, 14

The images in this book are reproduced through the courtesy of: Toby Parsons, front cover, p. 1; Alexandre Prevot/ Wiki Commons, p. 3; classic topcar, pp. 4, 9 (engine, diffuser), 15, 16, 17; pbpgalleries/ Alamy, pp. 4-5, 11; Unknown/ Wiki Commons, p. 6; Ev. Safronov, pp. 6-7 (left); Dan74, pp. 6-7 (right); Julia Lav, pp. 8-9; VanderWolf Images, pp. 9 (isolated), 14 (width); Artur_Nyk, p. 9 (steering); Novitec Rosso/ Wiki Commons, p. 10; Aflo Co. Ltd./ Alamy, p. 12; Dmitry Eagle Orlov, pp. 12-13, 14; Matti Blume/ Wiki Commons, pp. 14-15; Jack Skeens, pp. 18-19 (left); Marton Szeles, pp. 18-19 (right); Jarlat Maletych, pp. 20-21 (left); Dmitry Orlov/ Alamy, pp. 20-21 (right).